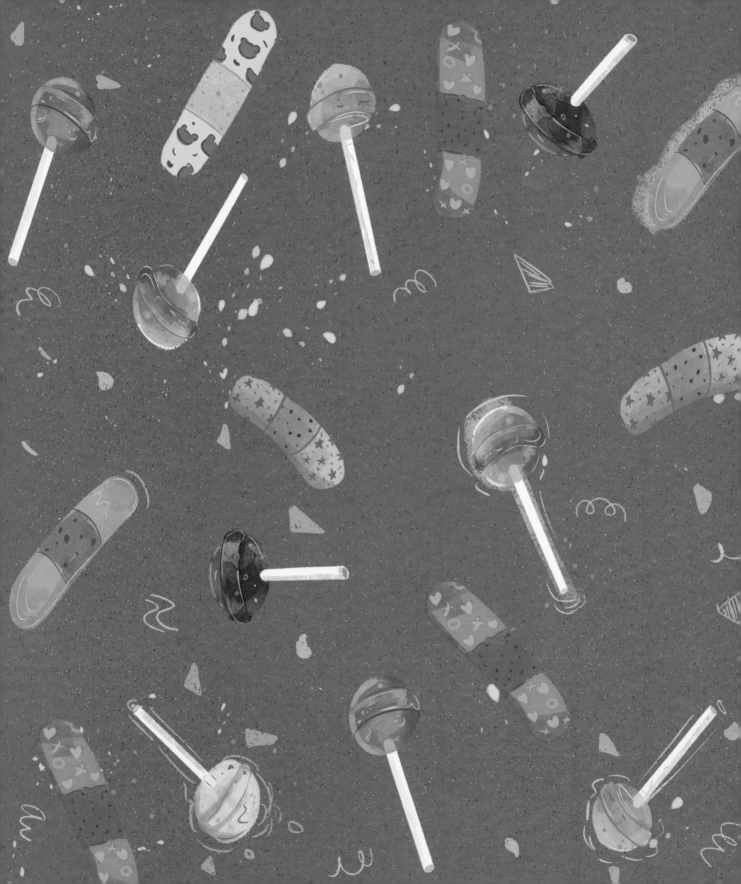

Maxine's Critters Get the Vaccine Jitters

Jan Zauzmer

Illustrated by
Corlette Douglas

THE EXPERIMENT
NEW YORK

MAXINE'S CRITTERS GET THE VACCINE JITTERS
Copyright © 2022 by Jan Zauzmer
Illustrations copyright © 2022 by Corlette Douglas

The Experiment, LLC
220 East 23rd Street, Suite 600
New York, NY 10010-4658
theexperimentpublishing.com

THE EXPERIMENT and its colophon are registered trademarks of
The Experiment, LLC.

The Experiment's books are available at special discounts when purchased in bulk for premiums and sales promotions as well as for fund-raising or educational use. For details, contact us at info@theexperimentpublishing.com.

Library of Congress Cataloging-in-Publication Data available upon request

ISBN 978-1-61519-838-2
Ebook ISBN 978-1-61519-839-9

Cover and text design by Beth Bugler

Manufactured in China
First printing January 2022

10 9 8 7 6 5 4 3 2 1

To Bob, Julie, Ben, Emily, and Mom—
I am pleased, as pleased as punch,
because I love my family a whole big bunch!
—J. Z.

I'd like to dedicate this book to my
family and friends who have always
supported me in my art career.
—C. D.

"Big news!
Grab your shoes."

"Each and every pet,
we're off to the vet
for a vaccine you need to get!"

Maxine told her critters . . .

as they got the jitters.

"It's okay to be fearful
and maybe a bit tearful—
very soon you'll feel cheerful,"

she said
as their dread
started to spread.

Under the bed
where they fled,
her pets didn't budge,
not even a nudge.

The finch
didn't flinch,

the hound
made no sound,

the pooch
didn't scooch,

and the kid
hid.

Would Scott
get a shot?
He sure hoped not.

Would Kay
get a spray?
Nope, not today.

And what about a booster
for Brewster the rooster?

Something smelled fishy.
Their mood turned to wishy—
you might tack on washy.
This scary plan they wanted to squashy.

But Maxine wasn't shy
about telling them why:

"It's no fun to get sick,
as sick as a dog—
or for that matter,
a hog or a frog."

"Let's let out a cheer!
The science is clear,
as clear as a bell:
Vaccines keep us well!"

They knew this was smart
and straight from her heart,
so to the vet
went every pet:

the kitten
called Mitten,

the filly
named Milly,

the fawn known as Dawn, and the foal dubbed Cole.

The office was clean,
as clean as a whistle—
no reason to bristle.

In they all scurried,
more or less worried.
Some even hurried!

Jervis
was nervous.

Franky
was cranky.

Dave
was brave.

Cary
was wary.

And Lucky the ducky
was ever so plucky.

Biffy
was iffy.

Freddy
was ready.

The vet was quick,
as quick as lightning.
This visit wasn't quite so frightening.

In fact, it was easy,
as easy as pie.
Not one creature began to cry.

Not a shout
from the trout,

not a plea
from the bee,

not a peep
from the sheep.

Nobody quit;
they all had grit.
No need to be grouchy
about this little ouchy!

Maxine was pleased,
as pleased as punch.
She loved her pets
a whole big bunch.

And now they were fit,
as fit as a fiddle.
But Maxine's busy day
was still in the middle. . . .

At three o'clock
she skipped to the doc

around the block.

One more vaccine—
this time for Maxine.

It was a cinch,
a super fast pinch!

Then without any jitters
she went home to her critters . . .

where she gave them all snacks—
a treat for getting their vax!

JAN ZAUZMER is the author of *If You Go with Your Goat to Vote* and *Maxine's Critters Get the Vaccine Jitters*. A graduate of Princeton University and Stanford Law School, Jan lives with her husband near Philadelphia, PA, where they raised their three children. She hopes that this book is a shot in the arm for kids at vaccine time.

CORLETTE DOUGLAS knew from a very young age that all she ever wanted to do was draw. She loves creating whimsical images of POC kids and silly animals that deliver a blast of colors and fun chaos on every page. Corlette is a born-and-raised resident of Brooklyn, NY.

corcorart.squarespace.com

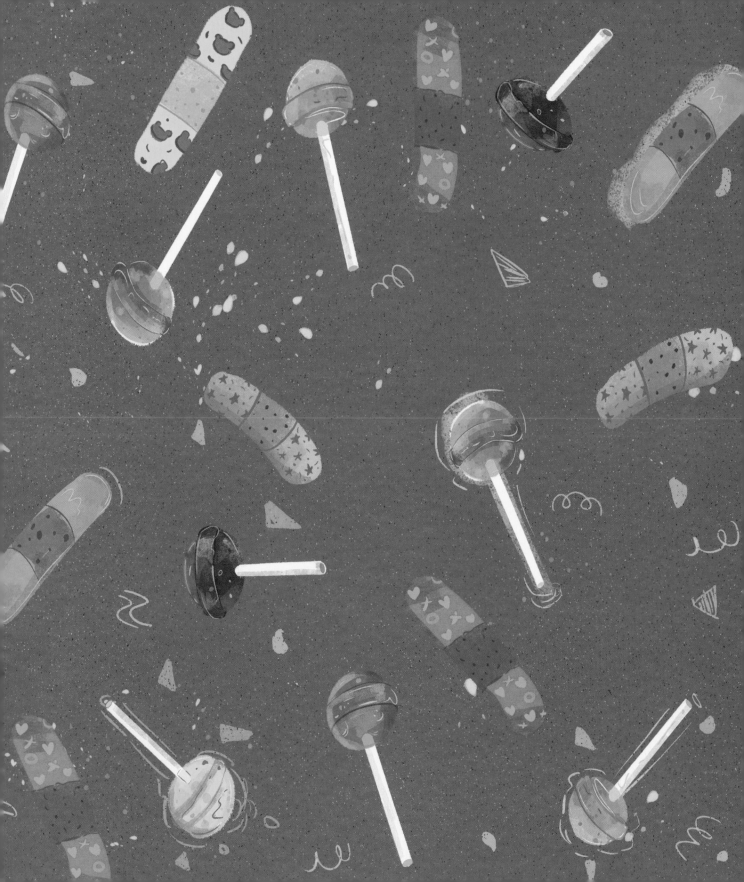